Born and raised in South Devon, Jill Nutbeem attended a secondary modern school until her education was complete. She went on to attend a technical college, where she undertook a two-and-a-half-year pre-nursing course to enable her to begin training as a state registered nurse at the age of eighteen. Qualifying in this at the age of twenty-one, she spent two years working in her training hospital, St John's in Chelmsford, Essex. She temporarily retired to begin a family and had two daughters.

To Shelley, who listened interestingly to the outpouring, by me, of the content of the book.

Jill Nutbeem

THE DEPARTURE LOUNGE

AUSTIN MACAULEY PUBLISHERS®
LONDON • CAMBRIDGE • NEW YORK • SHARJAH

Copyright © Jill Nutbeem 2025

The right of Jill Nutbeem to be identified as the author of this work has been asserted by the author in accordance with sections 77 and 78 of the Copyright, Designs and Patents Act 1988.

All rights reserved. No part of this publication may be reproduced, stored in a retrieval system, or transmitted in any form or by any means, electronic, mechanical, photocopying, recording, or otherwise, without the prior permission of the publishers.

Any person who commits any unauthorised act in relation to this publication may be liable to criminal prosecution and civil claims for damages.

This is a work of fiction. Names, characters, businesses, places, events, locales and incidents are either the products of the author's imagination or used in a fictitious manner. Any resemblance to actual persons, living or dead, or actual events is purely coincidental.

A CIP catalogue record for this title is available from the British Library.

ISBN 9781035873784 (Paperback)
ISBN 9781035873791 (ePub e-book)

www.austinmacauley.com

First Published 2025
Austin Macauley Publishers Ltd®
1 Canada Square
Canary Wharf
London
E14 5AA

I would like to thank Jackie and other members of Tyspane staff who assisted me with difficulties within my computer, where I am pretty illiterate.

'In the beginning, all that should have been was not'

Who would have guessed that a routine connecting flight to Guatemala in Central America, a country south of Mexico, was anything but easy? Home to rainforests, volcanoes and ancient Mayan sites, this country appealed not to the fainthearted but to those with a dramatic sense of adventure, drawing many to study the early ancient civilisation of this fascinating country, untouched for centuries but still available to the curious.

The eighty travellers were content to wait patiently to be called through to board the aircraft positioned on the tarmac, ready to receive its passengers for the long-haul flight to Guatemala. Airline crew were constantly on the alert for stragglers and boarding pass fraudsters, but for now, all was calm, with hostesses ready and waiting for the signal to begin the boarding procedures to seat their passengers accordingly. It would be a long journey, and the eighty expectant passengers would need all the skills and attention required of a trained airline host or hostess.

Having been equipped for all eventualities, it came as no great surprise when the overhead lights in both the aircraft cabin and walkthrough failed. Annoying but not irreversible, a temporary blackout no doubt, and emergency lights would soon come on whilst repairs were underway. Two or three minutes passed as blackness covered the entire airport. Consternation grew as urgent messages were transmitted across the terminal. No terrorist attack or armed robbery was reported by the security guards, as all the electrical engineers were working flat out to rectify the major fault. Alt activity in and around the airport was suspended, being closed for all purposes, flights included.

Suddenly, a scream was heard above the business of those doing their level best to restore the power–a panicky scream that the departure lounge was gone–disappeared into thin air, and the eighty passengers it held waiting to board the aircraft. It was inconceivable but true as officials gazed in dismay at the empty location of where the departure lounge should have been. How was this possible? An area the size of a small house couldn't just disappear, or could it? What about the passengers? Are they harmed? Personnel, the police, the army and the disposal experts were called in to look for what–a disappeared departure lounge. Impossible–must be shrouded in a mist that could have gathered after the lights went out, but there wasn't any evidence of a mist anywhere else in the airport. This can't be happening? How do we explain the disappearance of the eighty travellers in the lounge to friends and relatives?

Fear gripped the hearts of every person in the airport as the full extent of the tragedy sunk in. Could it be some sort of interference with cybernetics–artificial intelligence–engaging in some criminal activities? Had a machine been manufactured, and if so, what powerful machine could effectively lift the departure lounge from where it should be in the airport? Could it materialise again? Is there some form of control between animals and machines that could account for this phenomenon, and who would specialise in this knowledge? Counterintelligence was as aghast and horrified as everybody else, as never in all their experience had something like this happened before. Crack teams were swiftly promoted to explore every and any possibility. What could anyone do? How to find and bring back the departure lounge? Nobody knew the answer as, with heavy hearts and utter bewilderment, they gazed at the empty space where the departure lounge should have been located.

Steve and Juliet sat close together, surrounded by the hand luggage, sandwiches and guidebooks they were intending to use whilst sightseeing in Guatemala, when a slight shudder made them glance at each other. A small earth tremor but surely not here in rural England? None of the other seventy-eight passengers seemed at all perturbed, eagerly awaiting to be allowed on-board the intercontinental aircraft on which they would travel first to the USA, then a change to another airline taking them on to Guatemala City, a pivot for their reason to travel to this Central American country. Hopes for a turbulence-free, uneventful flight were running high tempered with excitement if, like Steve and Juliet, they were looking forward to the adventures Guatemala had to offer.

More shudders followed, feeling somewhat like a twisting motion, which did cause heads to be raised and a question or two to be asked. Another moment and a flight attendant came to alley them of any anxiety regarding these strange movements. Doors were closing, and the attendant disappeared from view. Steve released Juliet's hand, making his way to the point of entry to the departure lounge, but that door, too, was tightly closed. Other passengers were attempting to open the fire doors but to no avail. They were trapped and locked in. Nobody spoke for a moment, then various nervous half-hearted suggestions were made which made no sense at all. Some tried banging on the doors, again to no avail, others shouting for help until they fell silent from the sheer effort. What was happening? Could there have been a major earthquake or was the airport under siege?

A stunned silence followed the initial shock of being unable to escape from whatever was causing these disturbing movements, until then a very ordinary departure lounge in a very ordinary airport in Southern England. No rational explanation could be given, however, and the only thing to do was to try and remain calm and in control, expecting every moment to have the movements rationalised by an airport authority. Some of the passengers were crying uncontrollably being comforted by those nearby. AS Steve and Juliet sat solemnly holding hands, ready to help anyone if needed, there was a sudden lurch which appeared to tip the lounge on its axis, then moved away in a strange perpendicular direction from where they were before. Nobody had suffered any injury, only shock but this movement elicited more cries of terror. One by one dawned the recognition that they were still alive yet trapped in a moving sphere. Phones were switched on for any information coming from the outside world, although networks did not appear to be scrambling each other, with loud wails of distress coming from many a frightened passenger. Then, oddly, several families seemed confined in their own space, unable to move forwards or backwards. This was becoming more bizarre by the moment. Seeing the horror on each face and in their voices showed that much more was happening here than anyone had first thought. There were cries from other departure lounges across the world.

Suddenly, the phone lines became operable as cries of fear and alarm were heard from around the country and finally from across the world. Reports were coming in of entire office blocks shifting and shaking with the same movements the departure lounge was experiencing. Where were the networks to deal with what was happening? Were they immobilised or contained as all others seemed to be? Hospitals reported strange, oblique movements, but nobody suffered any injury, and operations were continuing as before. Trains, buses, and cars had their windows and doors sealed but were able to operate within limitations. It was desperately worrying, puzzling and frightening. Was a supernatural intelligence involved, and was the world subject to a powerful influence that could end the world as we know it? Speculation upon speculation was made, and some of those applied to those coming through the call channels. The police, who would normally deal with such extraordinary events, were themselves detained in police departments across the world, also scared and bewildered that their buildings, too, were moving in various directions. The occupants could not fully describe what was happening as they were contained in a box or cube minimalising outside movement from within the cube.

As Steve and Juliet sat with the others, each dealing with their fear and anxiety in their own particular way, when a voice was heard as if coming from a projector from behind a screen–a reasonable-sounding female voice asking for calm with a reassurance that nobody was going to be harmed in any way, only that was in restricted movements. The voice continued:

"Don't try to find out where I might be speaking from because you won't find me. I am in what you might call a parallel universe to yourselves. We need a lot from you. Our world is dying due to an over-exposure of cosmic debris from atomic energy emanating from another parallel or alternative universe closer to us than you are. The technology we use to defend ourselves has been drained, and we need to rebuild our dwindling supplies. The only way we can achieve this is to absorb all your data and technological advances you have made, to enable our world to survive. To enable us to do this we need to suspend you all in some way that would not incur any possibility of a retaliatory nature. You would not be able at any rate to direct any form of defence against our actions as we are invisible to you, and even your highly skilled interplanetary devices could not detect us. Nevertheless, we need this complete immobilisation as a deterrent against molecular structures in the atmosphere caused by movement outside the spheres that could detract from the correct procedures."

There was a stunned silence in the departure lounge, after which there were cries of: "You won't get away with this," and "We'll find and destroy you whoever you are. It's all lies– there are no parallel universes," and again "It's all fiction." Then silence fell once more whilst the passengers assimilated what they had been told, trying hard to make sense of it all but failing miserably. None of this made any sense. Finally, one or two advocated some form of escape, but there was no way out. Doors were locked, as were windows, and without any tools in the departure lounge, there wasn't any way to break free. Then the voice came again: "There isn't any way you can break free, but you can leave the room by walking through the walls. This time, you will meet with another sphere who will take you where you want to go–to the bathroom, for example, or to your home, but remember this: when you get home, you will also be in a cube or sphere." Again a stunned silence whilst this new piece of information was received and thoughtfully discussed. They could go home, not perhaps to a home they could remember, but a home encased in a sphere and captured by these aliens from an alternative realm or universe about to destroy our world by stealing our technology to avoid their world from being destroyed. What sort of position would that leave us in once they had taken all they needed? Bewildered once more by this second revelation but determined to test whether they could, in fact, leave the departure lounge, two couples walked resolutely to the lounge walls, disappearing completely, minus their hand luggage. A moment later, they returned with a strange story to tell. As they had passed through the walls of the departure lounge, they had encountered an empty space being forced to stop. A sphere the size of a small room had approached and engulfed them, enabling them to make for the bathroom. They could speak and be understood by those in the lounge as they said they had returned for their luggage and would be making their way homeward, intending to fly to Guatemala when this was over. A brave gesture but not for everyone, as groups of passengers sat huddled together, anxious and afraid of this new development. How could one walk through solid walls and in a sphere, for goodness sake?

    Steve and Juliet sat slightly apart from the others, wondering whether they could talk to the voice of whoever it was communicating these messages and find out who they were. A third time, the voice began to speak, conveying further instructions, but before much was said, Steve interrupted with a question: "We need to know if we can talk to you as you are talking to us now. We would like to understand who you are and what you are called. Being from an alternative reality to us, are you really us in a different time and space? Do you do and say the same things as us? Are you human? Do you look like us?" The voice came again, a little flustered this time:

"So many questions, but 'yes' you can communicate with us, and 'no' we don't do the same thing at the same time, but 'yes' there are comparative things that happen at different times. Essentially we are human but in a different way. You can call us HOMOGENUS or HOMOS when speaking to an individual such as myself, and if you're wondering if I'm male or female, I am in fact, in fact, female belonging to a large corporation of artificial intelligence designed millennia ago to interpret mankind's thinking and behaviour between our worlds. Until now, we have lived side by side with your world without any need to recognise or rely on one another in any way, but circumstances change, and we now need your technology. May I continue with our further instructions regarding travel plans?" Steve interjected, "Before you continue, I would like to ask you a further question. Why couldn't you have introduced yourselves to us and asked for our co-operation in saving your world?"

There was a distinct chuckle, then:

"Would you have believed anything we would have to say? Your world would have rejected the idea of an alternative universe, except perhaps for just a few. Your level of headiness would cause a huge barrier of disbelief and rejection. 'No' this is the only way." Steve was quiet as the voice continued: "If those of you who are left in this departure lounge would still like to travel to Guatemala, we can assure you that you can, but air flights are restricted to the same sphere dimensions as you are, although we can transport you there far quicker than your own aircraft would be able too. The sphere you're in will move forward in one of your moments, rotate, and then, at the speed of light, will have you in Guatemala in sixty of your moments. On your arrival, please remain seated, and I will tell you what to do next. Are you all happy about this? If not, you can leave with your luggage through the walls into another sphere and then be on your way. We have no desire to harm any human being."

Some passengers moved forward as if to leave, then changed their minds and sat down again. Still, others were in their huddles with whimpering sounds coming from the ladies. Steve and Juliet tried as hard as they could to alleviate their fears, but they were caught up in this as much as anybody, so they had few firm assurances to give other than to do as they had been requested. A moment later, the departure lounge lurched again, making a very definite rotating turn in an entirely different direction, then resumed its position, after which a gentle swishing noise could be heard until a light bump indicated they might have arrived. Waiting expectantly for Homos to address them, suddenly, a bright light came on, and a picture of Guatemala City appeared on a wall of the departure lounge. Alongside this appeared suggested visiting sites recommended by many travel advisers to be well worth a visit.

Steve and Juliet gazed at the picture, identifying the many areas they had planned to see, all of which would involve travel of some description, now seemingly impossible. But was it!

Homos spoke again and said, "We have arrived at Guatemala City, and those of you who want to visit this magnificent country may do so by walking through the walls of the lounge and into another sphere to take you on your journey." Steve spoke up not just for themselves but for everybody else.

"We and some of the other passengers would like to visit several sights involving various means of travel such as pony trekking, volcano hiking and other activities, but how do we manage when we are confined within these spheres? After what could only be assumed was a thoughtful pause, another voice, not Homos, declared that all these visits could be achieved, but the sphere cubes were to take each traveller where they wanted to go, but after each visit, they must return to the departure lounge where they would be given further instruction. Each time-lapse said the male voice would be minimal."

So began for those who had travelled to Guatemala for a particular reason, the most extraordinary holiday of their lives, being forced to see this country from the inside of the spheres in total isolation from even the Guatemalans encased in their own sphere cubes. Nobody moved for a while, consulting their travel documents and reviewing their lists of sought-after sites to visit. Guatemala, with its many fascinating buildings and local Mayan culture, was a definite must, but many of the tourists seemed reluctant to take the first move through the sides of the departure lounge to be enveloped in the sphere-cube on the other side. It was a very scary moment, and Steve and Juliet, although apprehensive themselves, decided to take that first step outside the weird setup to see the country that they had planned to see for so long. Walking swiftly, hand in hand, with a tour guide in their pocket, they reached the side walls of the departure lounge and then walked straight through to be halted in a dark space before a strange object approached, encasing them. Able to breathe and talk they observed the object was indeed like a sphere with a round top and bottom but with cube-like features of having corners and a flat top. The oddest-shaped form of transport they had ever seen.

Setting off in the right direction towards the city, Steve and Juliet needed to use a bus to transport them further into the city. As the sphere-cube moved in accordance to destination the bus took on a strange approach. Slipping from their original sphere onto the bus, that shape once more enclosed them, and they found a seat. Everywhere one looked were startled, apprehensive faces, but gradually, people moved around as they disembarked at their destination. Entering Guatemala City Steve and Juliet's attention was immediately focused on the horse cowboys and their magnificent mounts, they themselves enclosed in the sphere-cubes. Splendid buildings were in abundance, each exhibiting a degree of Mayan culture–an ancient civilisation here in Guatemala. It was a magical city if very odd for the occupants, and visitors had to walk in an entirely new way in their prison enclosures. Unable to communicate outside one's own sphere was a difficulty only remedied by sign language and to some degree, body language.

Shopping was impossible as nothing could be exchanged from within each sphere-cube. Steve and Juliet could only stand and admire the magnificent woven fabric that the we

Guatemalans produced without handling or purchasing a sample. At this loss of personal touch was discovered for themselves by the tourists there was a look of shock and dismay on many faces. On the central Plaza Mayor, the Metropolitan Cathedral was a visit Steve and Juliet wanted to make, so within their sphere-cubes, the pair made for the sight described in the guidebook and found, to their delight, that it was full of colonial paintings and religious carvings that they had not seen before. Another building they had wanted to visit was the National Palace of Culture–an imposing building that had a balcony overlooking the main square; it was grandiose with a magnificent facade and, with its construction lasting for hundreds of years, was a sight to behold. Many of its 350 halls are open to the public–the most famous being the Salado Recepcion where the country's most important ceremonies are held and boast a huge Bohemia crystal chandelier which, when all its lights are on one can see three million gold figures of the rare national bird of Guatemala–the Quetzal.

From many of the streets in the city, splendid views of volcanoes could be seen, with the highly coloured buildings on either side of the street giving a spectacular overview of this highly decorative city. Tiring now, Steve and Juliet would have liked a rest with a chance to sample some typical Guatemalan cru-sine, but this seemed to be impossible from within their sphere-cubes, so they decided to return to the departure lounge to see if anything could be rectified. All the sightseers would soon become dehydrated and, besides, would need to use the bathroom at some point. A few others from the departure lounge were returning, some like Steve, to negotiate with Homos or 'the voice' to see what provisions, if any, for their captives were available so they would be able to eat and drink. To have everyone die at this stage would surely not further the cause for the Homos, and besides, their captives had said that they did not want to cause harm to anyone.

Entering the lounge through the walls, dispensing with the sphere-cube that they had been enveloped in to see the sights of Guatemala City, they were now back in familiar territory. Steve addressed what appeared to be a small rectangular receiver protruding from a wall, beginning by saying,

"We've enjoyed our visit to Guatemala City now, finding ourselves hungry and thirsty. You yourselves have said you don't want to harm any of us, but hunger and thirst produce dehydration, which in return can cause death. I fail to see how this will help you in your endeavour to steal our technology. We need food and drink. Can you supply this, or must we fall ill and die? Can we return to the city to find these resources in some way? We also need to know where we'll sleep tonight. In our hotels?"

Homos returned the question immediately by saying;

"You're right. We have no intention of causing individual harm, and by limiting your access to nourishment for your bodies, we are in danger of destroying you. You see, we don't need that kind of intake as our bodies work differently to yours. Our means of keeping our bodies healthy is by the infusion of a gas each day–a gas that would kilt homo sapiens in a matter of hours. Your need for food and liquid must be considered paramount. You may partake of these nutrients by exchanging one sphere-cube for another, where food and drink are supplied by the occupier of that sphere-cube.

"We will watch that you all have your fair share, and tomorrow, we will re-access the availability of food and drink.

By the way, we fully appreciate the difficulty around your world of the fear generated by our stipulations and can only hope you can all adjust as quickly as possible. The extraction of your technology may take some time. The question of your sleeping arrangements must remain as we have indicated. Go to your booked hotels, and as you enter to check in, you will again exchange your arrival sphere-cube for the sphere-cube in that hotel. You will need to stay within that sphere-cube wherever to go in that hotel, and again, as you leave, you will be assigned another sphere-cube to take you to your next destination. Enjoy Guatemala."

Looking around the departure lounge, Steve saw some of the incredulous looks of dismay at having their movements so restricted, but at least some things had been made clear, and that was that they could now eat and drink in their places of residence. Although what was happening was entirely against man's freedom of choice, they did know a little of what they were up against. They had no option but to comply. Were these powers out there able to obstruct what was happening or was the entire world at the mercy of the HOMOGENUS from the ultimate reality nobody ever knew existed and who even now stealing everything that had taken generations to accumulate?

Many of the passengers of the departure lounge, including Steve and Juliet, feeling decidedly faint from lack of fluids, turned towards the lounge walls and, on passing through, were transported in their own spheres towards Guatemala City once more, enabling them to find a restaurant suiting their taste in food and drink. Before too long Steve and Juliet spotted a Thai and Guatemalan restaurant offering a selection of food and locally made drink, usually a type of beer that had suited their palates. Stopping outside, they went to enter the shop when they found themselves transported through the walls encased in a larger sphere-cube that contained the restaurant dining area and kitchens presided over by the owner, who, with a smile, welcomed the pair into his space in the sphere-cube indicating for them to sit down and offering the menu. Tired now, they complied, taking the offered menu. Choosing their favourite Thai meal, they eagerly waited for it to be prepared, at the same time indulging in a local Guatemalan drink to quench their parched throats, wondering how the other diners were faring with their extraordinary means of eating out. Life was so very strange now that nothing could be taken for granted.

Remembering the instructions to return to the departure lounge if wanting any further excursions, Steve and Juliet settled the bill after an excellent meal, the same way they had entered, encased once more in yet another sphere-cube, returning them to the departure lounge where they re-entered to request a volcano walk. The one they had chosen was the Pacaya Volcano, around a two-hour hike from the trailhead to the lava fields, which was an active volcano south of the capital. Their hotel in Antigua would be for a welcome rest when they returned. Only half the lounge was being used as a transit point as many were still out, taking in the many wonderful sights Guatemala had to offer. Feeling better after their meal, Steve and Juliet once again left the departure lounge to team up with the excursion to the volcano there, meeting with like-minded tourists intent on enjoying the never before visit to an active volcano. Each single pair or group of tourists were encased in their sphere-cubes, and although this means of travel was so very new, yet people were beginning to adapt rather than give up the opportunities to see the sights. Some grumbled at the intrusion on their privacy, while others speculated on the various news bulletins they had heard regarding the invasion or takeover, and the authorities who claimed it was all under control, their appeal to be calm and the promises that by tomorrow everything would be returning to normal, with a command not to be frightened. Also being announced was the fact that any references to the theft by the aliens of stealing our advanced technology to save their world was, in fact, a lie and not to be believed. This all seemed very reassuring, but Steve and Juliet were not convinced by anything they heard through the national or local press. As far as they were aware, the entire world was encased in these prisms, allowing movement, yes, but with very little room to manoeuvre or control what was happening in reality. It was certainly very frustrating to witness these very strange events and yet unable to prevent the loss of everything that held the modern world operating its daily source of life within its homes, offices, factories, schools and hospitals, for example.

The excursion to Pacaya volcano proved to be very successful, with the mainly young people even joking about their unusual means of getting around, although there were many local folk who were still baffled by what was causing this odd phenomenon, some of whom were not even aware of the announcement earlier by the HOMOGENUS, to a hushed and speculating world. Searching for the first hot spot of volcanic movement under the supervision of the guide revealed several new vents in the crusty surface but none causing imminent danger. Steve and Juliet thought the two-hour hike well worth the effort to reach the starting off point, which had to be reached by a local bus, called 'the chicken bus' for two reasons; the first because the chickens were sacrificed to the volcano god, the second because of the chicken crates, and subjected to the same sphere-cubes mode of travel. Existing their sphere-cubes to step onto the bus driver and passengers were encased in another cube containing them all. As the driver pulled away from the curb, he gave a wry smile, smoothly guiding the bus in its encasement. They had been driven to the site where the tour guide met them to where the lava flow was apparent to see. The experience was breathtaking. Returning the same way, Steve and Juliet left the bus at Antigua and, once in their new sphere cubes, made their way to their hotel, booking into a room that had a magnificent view of the volcanic scenery around them. Quickly unpacking, they made their way to the bar to have a drink, still meeting unhappy, uncertain guests, obviously not fully aware of what was going on and what to do next. These people may have only heard a garbled explanation of the events of the past day and were even now discovering the sphere-cubes they were continually walking into, becoming frightened and confused. The pair stopped to help wherever they could, offering reassurances and relevant information.

On reaching the restaurant of the hotel Steve and Juliet were shown an acceptable seating area sitting together to await the menu. Looking around, they saw many evening diners looking decidedly uncomfortable in their sphere-cubes that they had transferred into after leaving their hotel rooms, bars or even within the hotel itself when they could have been using the hotel pool for example, enjoying a massage or even having a game of pool. The transfer of personal bubbles would have been the same, and although the message across the world was given in all spoken languages, there would still be countries where the inhabitants did not understand the announcements. It was still early days, and international sources for people to ask for help in interpretation had yet to be set up due to the general sense of despair, dismay, disbelief and confusion which was paramount to every human being trapped in the mindless attempt to extract human technology and where did the adversary intend to begin? The human mind retained much of today's information the parallel world wanted, so would they resort to draining the minds of senior scientists of technology in the world? It was a delicate question to ask and put events on an even more difficult basis than before. These thoughts would continue to express themselves, especially when everyday activities were so uncertain and life itself had changed for citizens of every country of the world completely outside human comprehension.

The menu appeared to be a very comprehensive range of much-resourced numbers of dishes, including many local delicacies, of which the Mayan-inspired chicken stew was amongst the most popular.

Prior to the visit to Guatemala, Steve and Juliet had decided to be as adventurous as possible in their manner of eating. Returning to their room after a typical Guatemalan meal, the pair opted for a little television which covered the happenings of this extraordinary day, which barely seemed to be twenty-four hours since the time of the first announcement. A lot had happened since then, not less the Guatemalan sights they had managed to accomplish despite the obvious restrictions. With no further news, they made themselves a drink before bedtime before closing the blinds and sinking into the soft downiness of the duvet and mattress, quickly falling into a blissful slumber. As the room contained an en-suite, a visit to the bathroom posed no problem as there wasn't the necessity to change from one sphere-cube to another. Sleeping was easy as the sphere-cube conformed to the shape of the body, and breathing was light and comfortable despite the confines. Breakfast the following day was in a smaller room than the dining room of last night. The meal was of the self-service variety involving one sphere-cube change since leaving their room. As of last night, many guests were struggling with their restrictive cubes asking for help from the management who were themselves having their own difficulties. Again, Steve and Juliet offered help in any way they could, mainly to show calmness within the compliance of the sphere-cubes. There was little else anyone could do until the authorities had gained some control over the perpetrators of this deadly attack. Radios were blaring in most of the rooms of the hotel, with each guest anxious to hear the latest reports, which only gave a repartition of yesterday's warnings and instructions to the populace. Even the world's leading scientists were silent after promising yesterday that all was well and they were in control. What was being heard was lie after lie, and what would normally have been a busy, bustling town was now silent, with businesses and transactions still taking place but in a sober and frightened manner. Many Guatemalans remained indoors waiting for any news, unsure how to proceed. The hotel staff went about their daily chores resignedly and rather apathetically, preferring to be at home.

After breakfast, Steve and Juliet left the hotel with several others from the departure lounge to return there in their newly acquired sphere-cubes to request another sight-seeing tour, this time for Steve and Juliet to a Mayan archaeological building site where the ancient Mayans built and sculpted the magnificent temples of their era and where archaeologists and anthropologists would swarm for the opportunity to discover the first evidence of Mayan life many thousands of years ago. Tikal appeared to be the most popular of these sites, so the pair opted for these ruins. Considered the most impressive of many cities in central America, Tikal is situated in the northern rainforest region of Guatemala, now Tikal National Park and the ruins they were about to see were of the earliest Maya civilisation of the lowlands where agriculture was practised, stone buildings were built alongside pyramid temples and copper and gold was excavated. A form of hieroglyphic writing was developed that has largely now been deciphered. Sculpted heads of Mayan Deities were to be seen in many buildings–mainly sun, moon, rain and corn deities. Human sacrifice and blood-letting in the temples were evident. The people had also developed a type of paper.

Those travellers who wished to visit Tikal and other Mayan sites were given permission, but because the sites were some distance from Guatemala City, the best way to travel was by taking a local flight, again subjected to the form of seclusion by the use of the sphere-cubes that were still causing a lot of people fear and anxiety. Exiting the departure lounge via the walls was now almost becoming second nature, and as Steve and Juliet made their way to the airport, purchasing a return flight to Tikal a few other travellers decided to follow suit. The rather disturbed airline pilot was astonished that his plane was subject to the same rules of exclusion as everyone else, taking off as expertly as if he was unencumbered by a sphere-cube. After an hour's flight to Tikal, a further local bus took the sightseers to the first example of Mayan architecture, which was the ruin of a typical Mayan dwelling complex. After admiring the temples devoted to offering sacrifices to their specific deity and hearing about the blood-letting rituals, they marvelled that the engraved sculptures were magnificent for a civilisation living 2,000 BC and 4,000 years ago. Steve and Juliet wondered what tools they might have used for such precision work. On reading the guidebook, they soon realised that, in fact, in the first millennium BC, Mayan artists began to sculpt in stone, stucco, wood, bone and shell, also firing clay using mainly stone tools, devising realistic portraits of divine Lords, courtly looking captives and the most recent deities that they were admiring intensely. Mayan artisans were also skilled in making pottery. The firing of these clay balls was used in the preparation of food placed directly onto the pots of food to cook and had been used in pots before adding meat, corn salt and spice. They seemed to have rejoiced in quantity. It was an enlightening time for Steve and Julie despite the enclosing confines of the sphere-cubes they had been forced to wear.

After viewing and exclaiming over many unbelievable but memorable pieces of artefacts, the day was soon turning towards evening, and they didn't want to miss the flight back to Guatemala City, so began their long journey tired but immensely glad they had made the flight having only just discovered that the bus journey would have been a nearly eight-hour ride and in the circumstances would have been very uncomfortable if not impossible. As it was, it had been a tiring day, and as they made their way back to their hotel, they were looking forward to a nice cold, locally made beer.

Discussing, over the evening meal, the events of the day, their other excursions and the fact that there had been no meaningful announcements from HOMOGENUS about their intention to extract all technology from planet Earth, Steve and Juliet reflected on how Guatemalans were responding to the sphere-cube restrictions. They did note that although the children were exempt from having to move within the spheres, they found it difficult to acclimatise to their parents' situation, often returning crying and distressed to these parents who did their best to reassure and encourage, although often they themselves did not fully understand. After another enjoyable meal and a day spent amongst the Mayan ruins of Tikal, the pair retired early to their room to listen for further reports of the day. As the weather was warm, promising to be so for the next few days, Steve and Juliet had decided to spend the following day at the hotel–sunbathing by the pool and taking advantage of the in-house activities such as massages and the use of a games room. They also needed to report back to the departure lounge as in another four days' time, their adventurous holiday in Guatemala would be coming to an end, and they would have to contemplate the return flight to the UK via New York. They were about to find out how the world was coping with this global situation.

Once more studying the guidebooks, Steve and Juliet wanted to plan for the day after tomorrow, and with the many attractions on offer, they wanted to maximise all they could see of this wonderful country. For example, the resplendent Quetzal–the national bird of Guatemala, also their named currency–was a protected species and, with an image bearing its name, seemed to have a particular significance in the country. Found in the rainforests of Guatemala, blending well with the foliage with its bright green colouring and magnificent long tail, probably with which to draw a mate, this bird, for the ancient animistic Mayans, was thought to be a spirit guide and highly revered. It is now shown on the national flag of Guatemala. It would certainly be well worth a visit to see if one could spot them in a wildlife reserve near Coban, an area not too far from Guatemala City, which sadly has a high drug-related crime rate and a poor justice system with cartels keeping the country of Guatemala poor, certainly amongst the indigenous people of this country where poverty is high.

Following a leisurely day at the hotel, the pair returned to the departure lounge, where they arranged a day at the wildlife reserve, hoping they might spot the Quetzal, now an endangered species due mainly to the loss of its natural habitat by the destruction of the rainforests. Whilst in the departure lounge with several other tourists arranging visits, Steve addressed the voice system of the HOMOGENUS, asking for the latest situation regarding their intentions to be informed that the planned procedures were taking place but not yet completed, reporting that there had been a severe interruption by a global team of experts in the field of technology who had attempted to disperse the shields surrounding everything that moved so temporarily preventing the extraction of the technology they needed. This act of rebellion was seen as espionage, and the perpetrators were punished.

"We are angry," said the voice for all to hear, and although it said we don't want to harm anybody, "we will retaliate if our business is thwarted again in any way. We will, however, allow the excursions today, but tomorrow and the following days until the end of your time in Guatemala, you are to report twice a day to the departure lounge to account for your movements."

Seeing upset faces of consternation amongst their fellow travellers, Steve and Juliet did their best to console and encourage broken-hearted people to be brave, and somehow they would all come through this together. Even now, they reasoned scientists would be exploring all the possibilities of bringing this threat to an end releasing all of us forced to submit to wearing these sphere-cubes, restricting our movements. A few were crying, some angry, fearful and anxious, being comforted by relatives. One or two began to make their way to the side walls of the departure lounge, disappear through to be collected by their sphere-cube, ready to begin the chosen excursion for that day.

Steve and Juliet followed swiftly enough ready for their visit to the wildlife nature reserve to Corban, their structures surrounding them as they made their way to where the now familiar chicken buses were waiting for passengers. As the driver appeared nonplussed with the arrangements, he seemed in no particular hurry to drive, although quite a few passengers were already on board, not all bound for the wildlife reserve, some with chickens in crates ready to journey to a local market. Steve decided to ask the driver why he wasn't pulling away despite being full, to be told that because of the sphere-cubes they were putting his bus in danger and therefore he had to raise the fares, which the local people didn't like. Steve reasoned with him that if that was the way he really felt about the danger, then to talk reasonably with the passengers and explain the need to raise the fares perhaps by half the amount, then he thought they would comply. This the driver did with the desired result, and before long, they were on their way to Corban, a journey of about four hours, allowing for market stops along the way. Coban itself is in the coffee-growing region of Guatemala employing local Guatemalans as the main crop pickers. The nature reserve was to be found close to the town of Coban with the driver of the chicken bus being helpful in giving on-going directions from where he finally terminated the route.

In these highlands where Steve and Juliet found themselves, they were aware of the cloud overhanging the rainforest, the wetness that produced good coffee, and the noises as well as birdsong vibrating along the many trails to be found once in the wildlife reserve of Coban. Entering the reserve, they were immediately aware of exotic birds only to be found in the rainforest, but sadly, not the reserved Quetzal as yet. There was always time, though, as they searched for the giveaway long tail. Beautiful inland lakes were apparent, and in the distance, Steve and Juliet could hear what sounded like a waterfall. The guidebook had indicated that swimming was permitted, so they had both brought along suitable swimwear, which they hoped they would have the chance to use later on, but at the moment, the pair were taking in the wonderful tapestry of flora to be found in the rainforest. Suddenly ahead of them, a long green tail flashed, disappearing into the surrounding green shrubbery of the forest. It could only have been the Quetzal with that magnificent tail. Treading lightly now, Steve and Juliet walked with bated breath and a watchful eye when a pair of very definitely resplendent Quetzal flew directly across their path, seemingly in a hurry to find shelter or looking for a mate–now being the mating season. To see two of these colourful birds at such close proximity was a sight neither of them would forget. Walking now in the direction of a thunderous roar, they soon came across the source of the sound–a full-throated waterfall cascading downwards in its descent through the rainforest, settling into a tropical pool of blue water. The pair decided to rest in such a tranquil area, and finding a delightfully carved seat amongst the undergrowth, they opened their lunch boxes and cans of drinks to enjoy against the backdrop of the falls with a myriad of birds of many hues flitting across the magical tropical scenery. Lying back into the lushness of the undergrowth, the pair very soon found themselves nodding off, especially after their long bus journey that morning, when Steve suddenly sat up, wondering how they could swim encumbered within their sphere cubes. The only way to find out was, of course, to try, so after tidying up their residue of lunch, they tentatively waded into the water to find, to their surprise, that they were released from the cubes to enjoy the luxury of the pool's cooling waters. Swimming and diving in total freedom from the sphere-cubes, they frolicked like water babies, losing all track of time so engrossed were they in the joys of the rainforest and its inhabitants. Only when the sun began to dip across the horizon did they realise that the bus returning to Guatemala City may well have left Coban, and they could be stranded. Already out of the pool and finding themselves once more reluctantly re-enveloped in their sphere-cubes Steve and Juliet hurriedly retraced their steps towards the town of Coban, where they found the chicken bus had left half an hour before and wouldn't be returning until late the following afternoon.

In a strange town, but fortunately, with some quetzals between them, they weren't too perturbed beginning to make inquiries for rooms at what looked like small guest houses, but none had any availabilities as it was the town's twice monthly targe fair and market so all the rooms were accounted for. Some local children were playing together in what could only be the town square, so Steve asked, in broken Spanish, if any of them knew where they could find a room for the night. One child ran off, returning a few minutes later with an elderly Guatemalan, possibly his grandfather, who gesticulated with his hands for them to follow him. He was nimble, trotting quietly between the poorly constructed houses until he came to one on the outskirts of the town, looking a little better than those they had passed. Beckoning them to follow him inside, the elderly man stopped by the side of a young woman cooking on a dilapidated stove long past its best. Speaking rapidly to her in Spanish, Steve and Juliet could hear him explaining the situation, then turned to the young boy to relay an instruction; before making sure the pair had some quetzals with which to pay for the kindness, he rewarded them with smiles. The boy then showed them a room slightly apart from the main house and complete with fresh bed linen, inviting them then to a meal that would be served in the kitchen, in half an hour's time. What an invitation! Sitting at a rickety old table with the old man at the head, Steve and Juliet were served a basic but substantial meal followed by a delicious dessert and cold local beer, Juliet hoping that they hadn't caused the family to have more meagre portions than usual, by their late arrival. The two younger boys chattered away nonstop at the table whilst the old man and presumably the boy's mother engaged in a quieter discussion drawing Steve and Juliet in as far as possible. The friendliness shown was overwhelming, as was their generosity in allowing the use of the bedroom for the night. Juliet assisted afterwards with the washing up and clearing away, earning again another smile of gratitude from Moulee, the grandfather. Bedtime followed shortly for the two boys, and it wasn't long before Steve and Juliet, in broken Spanish, extended their goodnights too.

Their room was old and tired but perfectly clean, and once tucked in, the pair slept well with rainforest noises, bringing them to wakefulness when the sun rose. A jug of warm water and a basin had been thoughtfully left outside their bedroom door, so making full use of the commodities at hand, they prepared themselves for the day ahead when the chicken bus should arrive in the afternoon to take them back to Guatemala City and the departure lounge. Another trail in the rainforest seemed like a good idea, but this time, they must be more conscious of time and not miss the bus again. Returning the linen, jug basin and bowl back to the kitchen, Steve and Juliet found the family eating breakfast, having laid a couple of extra places. Sitting down, they were served a hearty meal, after which the boys hastily said goodbye and ran off in the direction of a building that could easily have been a school. Having settled for their overnight stay, Steve and Juliet outlined their plans for the morning, whereupon the boV's mother, Greta, insisted on giving them a packed lunch to eat before catching their all-important bus. Goodbyes and a sincere thank you, said Greta, showing the pair how to find the wildlife reserve again, leaving them to enjoy the morning's excursion.

Finding the new trial leading in a different direction from yesterday promising an even denser part of the rainforest where the canopy of the trees almost occluded the rays of the sun, with the trial becoming difficult to follow. Here, the noises from within the rainforest were deafening, with the shrieks and howls of the population very apparent. Vibrant flashes of colour indicated an abundance of bird life, and many times, the long green-tailed Quetzal could be seen. If one looked upwards towards the canopy, you could sometimes spot a bright green head, assuredly the owner of the flamboyant tail belonging to either one of the two species of the resplendent Quetzal. As with yesterday, many a flash of blue could be seen amongst the trees–these were ponds refreshingly cool to hot hikers intent on seeing all they could in their visit to this central American country of Guatemala. Enjoying their lunch by the side of one emerald pool deep in the rainforest Steve and Juliet finally glanced around to say goodbye to all this beauty, making their way back to Coban to meet the bus arriving from Guatemala City and returning the same evening. This time they arrived as the bus was pulling in, and on asking the driver what time they were returning to Guatemala that evening were informed it wouldn't be going back until tomorrow morning. Shocked at the thought of another night in Coban with hardly enough Quetzals left for the return fare Steve and Juliet looked blankly at each other. What should they do? In a dismayed state, they approached the driver to ask if they could spend the night on the bus as they hadn't any more Quetzals left with which to pay for a room if one was available. The driver recognised Steve from the previous encounter on the bus when he had wanted to raise fares and Steve had intervened on behalf of the passengers, bringing an easy resolution. Uneasily, he offered the use of the bus to Steve and Juliet, warning that Coban had its quota of teenage thefts and for them to be constantly on the alert. Gratefully accepting the driver's offer, Steve and Juliet clambered aboard.

Finding enjoining seats at the rear of the bus where they could stretch and flatten themselves out so as not to be seen so easily, thereby not inviting possible disaster from gang raiders on the lookout for an easy Quetzal from unsuspecting tourists, It was a long uncomfortable night for them both, trying to avert danger and sleeping very little. With a few scraps of their packed lunches left, they nibbled their way through the night, gratefully seeing the driver approaching the bus just before seven the following morning, thoughtfully carrying two cartons of piping hot coffee for his two invited stowaways. Pulling two packets of something from his uniform front pocket, he gave them to Steve and Juliet, who soon realised they contained tortillas or corn cakes, a basic food supply and a very welcome sight when hungry. This was followed by slices of papaya wrapped in a clean hanky. They were verbally thankful to their indirect host.

By eight o'clock, the bus was full of bustling passengers and squawking chickens in baskets en route to market on the way to Guatemala City. It promised to be a long, hot, dusty day, but the restrictions of the sphere-cubes didn't seem to dampen spirits, and once inside the single sphere-cube of the bus, the chatty village folk spread themselves in many directions to talk to friends and neighbours irrespective of how far away from their seats, they were.

Pulling into Guatemala City at lunchtime Steve and Juliet made it straight to their hotel room, which they hadn't yet vacated and where a welcome shower was awaiting them. Whilst away, they had been unable to receive any news on the part of the HOMOGENUS' worldwide ambush of the world's technology, being eager to be brought up to date but were disappointed to learn that nothing further had been reported since they had been away. Steve, however, carried a small remote receiver not available for use in the rainforest and tuned into a global station, hoping for a wider report and was delighted by what he heard. This was obviously hush-hush and gave him hope. What he did hear was in proportion to a light being switched on in a darkened room. Undetected by the HOMOGENUS of the alternative universe, and despite the restrictions caused by the sphere cubes, the world's top scientists had devised a plan to thwart the assimilation of the world's technology by the HOMOGENUS hell-bent on saving their world despite the odds. Our scientists had built two mega structure computers designed to exchange information interrelating with each other, their role being to take a particle of snow from the Antarctic and in the stratosphere many miles out in space where the hole in the ozone layer would act in our favour, combine the snow sample with created water theoretically 'seed' sow in the atmosphere which would then produce a profusion of snow around the hemispheres of Earth effectively preventing the atmospheric collection of all the world's high-class data and technology, relevant research and countless man-hours of striving for perfection from the intended stealing by protagonists from another realm leaving earth bereft and vulnerable to attack without any operational defences. At whatever the cost this dastardly act had to be stopped once and for all.

Sudden falls of snow, particularly in parts of the world closer to the equator, were an unprecedented occurrence, and with the outcome of snow never having been experienced before, it was a pretty radical happening for many. Particularly in the equatorial rainforests of the world, even a small amount of snow could kill thousands of animals and birds, some of which were protected species, but even this result had to be accepted in order to allow the world to retain its technology without which many people could not survive threatened by unknown microbes and viruses set to kill with nothing to stop the spread of these unknowns.

Steve was astonished and horrified by these proposals but applauded the efforts of these men of science determined to save the planet by whatever means they had at their disposal. Juliet was silent as she listened intently to the forthcoming attempt to ward off the imminent attack by the alternative universe. Making their way to the departure lounge, aware that this would be the last day of exploration for them and the end of their holiday in Guatemala, they encountered a chilly atmosphere when they arrived. They had obviously been missed. No sooner had they entered the lounge than the voice of a HOMOGENUS sounded across the area, addressing Steve and Juliet, wanting to know why they had been missing for the past two days, not reporting into the lounge like everybody else. Steve replied that they had failed to catch the bus from Coban returning to Guatemala City, and had therefore been delayed returning until this morning, conveying their apologies. Being asked why they hadn't reported in for the last two days, Steve replied that a failure on their part had prevented them from returning the same day with the chicken bus, finding themselves unable to return until this morning. This explanation appeared to be grudgingly accepted as the voice continued with the matters of the day, reminding the passengers that this would be their last sightseeing day before the departure lounge returned them the following day to the airport terminus where they had begun their journey. Steve then took it upon himself to enquire if their work on the planet was coming to an end and how soon would the world's population be realised from the necessity of the sphere-cubes to be informed that the extraction of the world's technology was a delicate issue and could not be hurried. The voice implied they were on target but the use of the sphere-cubes would have to be continued for a while yet. Disappointed, Steve voiced everyone's opinion that this was going on for far too long, and had they encountered any opposition from the global scientific experts to be told that anything like that was classified information and would not be discussed in the departure lounge, leaving Steve and Juliet wondering about the threatened snowfalls all over the world.

Whilst the remainder of the passengers decided what to do on their final day, Steve and Juliet put in a request to visit Antigua–a city in the southern/central highlands of the country, and where the volcano called Papaya was situated having visited it on the second day of their tour, they wanted to see more of the surrounding area. This was granted, and very soon, the pair were en route to the next bus that would take them to the colonial city of Antigua, which had plenty of attractions with which to draw the tourists, many of which were of local produce and the brightly coloured houses on both sides of the streets created a wonderful centrepiece to many pathways of interest including museums to a chocolate factory who were making excursions to caoba farms producing this and other commodities. The chocolate is grown organically in between the volcanoes where the soil is richest. The countryside surrounding the city was breathtakingly beautiful, with volcanoes in abundance, many of them being extinct. An artisan market was a must for Steve and Juliet, who took great pleasure in the local produce of decorative Guatemalan woven articles which caught the eye, some of which they purchased as gifts to take home and remembrances of their holiday in Guatemala.

Tired after their exhaustive walking around the streets and the market, the pair made their way to Central Park, where they sat and relaxed with an ice cream before having a light lunch. For the afternoon, a coffee tour was being advertised, so after catching yet another chicken bus, they rode to a farm where English was spoken being amazed at the process by which excellent Guatemalan coffee was produced, finally enjoying a mug of the famous brew before returning again on the chicken bus to Guatemala City from where they reported to the departure lounge in time to hear HOMOGENUS give instructions regarding their departure home the following day which was scheduled for 8 am in the morning. The HOMOGENUS would have known how many were in the lounge at the beginning of the flight and each passenger would be accounted for in the morning. They said they would allow a brief period for people to be a little late if catching buses or cabs, but if anybody were unable to get to the departure lounge, for instance, because of illness, they would be left behind to return home by another route when fully recovered. On arrival back in London the HOMOGENUS expected everyone to leave the departure lounge as quickly as possible as the airport would only be open for a short period of time to allow for evacuation, then the airport would be re-closed. Steve once again asked for further updates on the situation at hand and what to expect when in London but was again told that there would be no further announcements until the flight tomorrow, and London was in line with the rest of the world with sphere-cubes still being used.

Back at the hotel, Steve and Juliet, having finished their evening meal, decided to finish with a local alcoholic drink– a medium-strength lager before making their way upstairs. Once there, they weren't sure what time the office would be open in the morning to settle the bill, still allowing them to reach the departure lounge before 8 am, so Steve went to see if there was anyone around who would have access to the office. To his delight, the manager of the hotel was still in the dining room and was more than happy to open up the office. Finding the bill quite quickly, which Steve settled with a favourable tip of thanks for an enjoyable stay, they said their goodnights. Saying their goodbyes to the staff after breakfast wasn't easy for the pair as everyone had been so very kind and helpful, and Steve and Juliet were sad to be leaving but leave they must not before they vowed to return to this delightful country. The local chicken bus soon had them back at the departure lounge arriving in plenty of time for checking in. Many, with their luggage, arrived at 7.55 am when an announcement was made that in exactly five minutes, a movement within the departure lounge would be felt as before and rapid movement thereafter. In a fraction of the time of a commercial flight, they would be arriving at the airport terminal. Sure enough, the sliding and rotating motions happened as expected, followed shortly afterwards by a slight bump, then came the final announcement from the HOMOGENUS that they had now landed and to evacuate the departure lounge as swiftly as possible.

There was quite a crowd by the far wall but eventually, everybody plus their luggage made it through the walls. Without a backward glance at their strange mode of travel, the passengers said farewell to one another before merging into their sphere-cubes and into the London streets, whether to locate a taxi or walk to their places of residence. Steve and Juliet needed a taxi–no chicken buses here, making for the usual taxi rank outside the airport, but this was empty as all outgoing and incoming flights had been cancelled. A little perplexed, they wondered what to do until Steve realised he had some local taxis on his phone, and after a second call, a taxi company agreed to pick them up and return them to their home just outside London. On reaching home, they were astonished at the normality of hearing the telephone ringing from anxious family and friends enquiring if they were home safely from their trip to Guatemala. It had certainly been a never-to-be-forgotten holiday, but despite the obvious difficulties, Steve and Juliet had enjoyed many new and exciting things whilst reassuring anxious telephone callers that all was well and they were well and truly home, about to enjoy a cup of their favourite tea then unpack gradually.

Spreading their souvenirs and gifts on their bed, they relived many of their adventures–the sights, sounds, smells and vibrant colours of the country still very much alive in their memories, and how, in such a short space of time, they were home again. Looking at each other still in their travelling clothes, they wondered what the next step was going to be. Both had jobs to return to in the city but had no idea what the situation was regarding the sphere-cubes. Juliet worked in an office and would probably have to follow the same procedures as they had whilst on holiday, but Steve was a site manager moving frequently from place to place. He did wonder, though, whether building work may have had to be suspended due to the current crisis that held the world in its grip. Both had two more days of their annual leave left, so a few telephone calls should clarify things for the time being.

The following day London seemed as grid-locked as before but with the extraordinary sights of seeing people and cars encased in their sphere-cubes, running as efficiently as before. It appeared to Steve and Juliet that everyone was becoming acclimatised to their new way of getting around. Industry appeared to be thriving, and the population of London, at least, was determined not to give in to the HOMOGENUS's devious plans to devoid the planet of its technology, leaving vulnerable people all over the world in great distress. But what of these proposed plans Steve had heard about on his transistor radio whilst in their bedroom in Guatemala? From what the pair could see, the life of Londoners was continuing very much as before despite the restrictions covering every aspect of daily life. Regular bulletins were broadcast on the main stations, bringing an updated version of events, but none were explicit enough to reveal the true state of the emergency and what would happen when all the global technology had been extracted for use by the parallel universe. Would we, as homo sapiens, be left alive to continue an existence far removed from which it had known before, or would death be preferable at the hands of HOMOGENUS–the enemy we didn't know? It was a question on everyone's lips and a general topic of conversation not just throughout London but throughout the world.

While world leaders and governments seemed powerless to intervene with what was happening, at least one advantage was that restraints were being broken down between countries antagonistic towards each other, and a global peace descended whilst ways and means of stopping the seemingly inevitable were being considered by specialists in the field of electronic, nuclear, cosmic ideology fusion and the utmost top secret technological advances of all times being, without doubt, the ones looked upon to deliver the world from the mess it was in, getting more and more intense as the days and weeks increased without any fathomable answers to bring faith in science once again. All hope was being lost! No one knew when the danger was going to end, and so far, very few newscasts had been given by the HOMOGENUS, even to major governments. A silent enemy was probably worse than one uttering threats or proclaiming victory, and with the world not even knowing how great the danger was from day to day, every island and country in every part of the globe held its breath.

Juliet returned to work in the office of a recruiting agency with news to tell of a very strange holiday in Guatemala, engaging in long conversations about how they were transported there and their mode of travel whilst in the country. Equally, Juliet wanted to know how her friends had fared in London at the beginning of the assault on Earth. There were many amusing stories that were told, but underneath, Juliet was aware of the existing fear and anxiety regarding how the danger would end and what would become of them all. She felt and told them how very courageous she thought they were in being able to come to work each day, continuing with their various assignments enabling the agency to continue in its role of recruiting personnel into companies requiring employees. It seemed a logical way of dealing with the unknown, bringing a little sanity into everyday life.

Steve's role as site manager on a building complex was partially available to him as much work on the technical side of procedures and building regulations had to take place indoors, but a lot of the structural work at higher levels had been suspended due to the danger of the sphere-cubes snagging and workmen being put in danger. Foundations were still able to be dug with lower wall construction still taking place, so Steve was still required to oversee maintenance at ground level and work taking place within the offices. The men were intrigued with his description of Guatemala, the bizarre arrival within the departure lounge, and his and Juliet's movements whilst in the country, the magnificent volcanoes, the Mayan architecture and sculptor of Tikal, the colonial beauty of Antigua, the account of the night spent in Coban and the striking flamboyance of the rainforests residents particularly the long green tailed Quetzal bird dominating the colourfulness overall. Listening in on his transistor radio whenever possible, Steve hoped to hear more about the global scientists' endeavours to prevent the removal of all technology from planet Earth but heard little that raised any hope of success, until one day, on a highly secret transmission, Steve was ecstatic to hear that the computers had been built that would achieve the desired effect of snow high up in the stratosphere thirty-one miles above the Earth being the second layer of the atmosphere, the final layer being the exosphere located between 440 and 6,200 miles above the Earth's surface, merging with the solar winds. According to the scientists, this higher level of Earth's atmosphere need not be involved with the daring plan to have the stratosphere produce the amount of snow needed to envelop the Earth to a depth of at least five feet from pole to pole, blanketing all communication and the inevitable prevention of transmitting to the parallel world of the HOMOGENUS anything other than a small amount of technology not having the ability to prevent their world from being destroyed by the nuclear cosmic rays bombarding it. All higher technology would remain intact with mankind being saved. Steve relayed all this to Juliet when she came home from work that evening, and together, they celebrated.

Still, no word came from HOMOGENUS, and although the world's channels broadcast several times a day, there wasn't any progress in hearing that the HOMOGENUS had completed their extraction, were experiencing any difficulties, when the enclosing by sphere-cubes would end or if the people of Earth could expect a final emptying of all knowledge and understanding to pretty much obliterate mankind. Then, a few days after this secret transmission, Steve heard another report indicating that the beginning of the experiment was to take place the following day. The plan was to introduce icicles of snow taken from the Antarctic and, with the introduction of the computers to relate to each other cause generated water and with the ice particles produce a severe weather pattern of ice formation in the stratosphere, multiplying into massive sheets of snow ready to be deposited onto the earth from pole to pole bringing with it the desired depth to prevent the transmission of earth's higher technology. "By tomorrow evening," the reporter said, "we shall know if our radically made plans of stopping the HOMOGENUS has been a success or a dismal failure. There would not be a second chance; this was repeatedly broadcast on the secret channel, as failure would mean that all would be exposed, and those held responsible captured and possibly killed to stop any further attempts to prevent the extractions."

Both Steve and Juliet were at work the next day, but neither could speak of what they had heard. Hurrying home in the evening both were glad to be at home together to hopefully witness the end to human misery metered out by the HOMOGENUS. The air seemed definitely chillier, although it was May, and a warm spell had been forecast. Suddenly, on looking out of the window, a few flakes of what appeared to be snow fluttered to the ground, and then more raced through the leaden skies until, by now, it was snowing heavily. Steve and Juliet hugged each other, jumping for joy. Now was the time to find out if the proposed plan would work or not. Telephones began to ring from family and friends experiencing this strange phenomenon in May. The pair hastened to explain what they had heard over the secret transmissions that this was an experiment planned globally by scientists who planned this to happen to prevent any further technology from being extracted by the HOMOGENUS. There were cheers of anticipated success across the airwaves, and a little later on in the evening, the scientists were claiming an astounding victory as the heavy fall of snow from pole to pole had effectively stopped the extractions from continuing. Whilst the world rejoiced, it also awaited recriminations from the HOMOGENUS, which was soon forthcoming. Governments around the world were threatened with severe retaliation unless the impending further snowfall was stopped, by which time the enemy had reasoned that the huge amount of snow and the possibility of more to come was computer-generated and incredibly efficient in preventing the accumulation of all the technology they needed and hadn't yet procured.

Earth was locked in a mini-ice age, causing severe disruptions and inconveniences across the globe. Those worst affected were in the Southern Hemisphere nearest the equator, where snow had never been seen. Many homes were inadequate to deal with the low temperatures, with many people dying of exposure, as did many endangered species of mammal and birds living in the many rainforests of the world who again had never experienced snow and such low temperatures. Sadly exotic birds such as the quetzal in Guatemala were among the victims. We had retained our higher technology for the world but at such a loss. Righteous indignation reigned, and anger at the perpetrators was high who had caused such drastic action to be pitted against them. In return, the HOMOGENUS, who refused to abort their attempts to seize Earth's technology, restricted, even more, the movements of both individuals and all forms of traffic, bringing gridlock to all cities and towns reliant on some form of transport. Food supplies dwindled across the globe, especially supermarkets in the Western world, as supplies could not reach them. Farmers were forced to bring all livestock into barns and sheds, but as feed could not reach them, many died. And still, the snow continued with the ever-hopeful conclusion of surrender, but none came. Meanwhile, governments in their seclusion zones met and deliberated the situation, which was becoming more and more urgent to find an answer to the gridlock.

Gripped as it was by snow and severely low temperatures, the world was slowly dying, with the population fearing the worst outcome of slow starvation. Somehow, a resolution or some form of truce must be found to suit everybody's needs. An announcement on a worldwide news waveband was made one day that the governments of the world were going to approach the HOMOGENUS with a proposition to try to resolve this dreadful situation. Many resisted the idea and challenged the governments to think again before perhaps offering a relaxation of the weather situation in return for possible withdrawal from their side. Everything possible was being considered and needed to be instituted, so a deal was struck with an appropriate time and place for the world leaders to meet face-to-face with the HOMOGENUS with proposals for the continuing survival of both planet Earth and the parallel universe of the HOMOGENUS without which both planets could fall into extinction. The audacious proposal from Earth's governments and scientists from all over the world was to assist the HOMOGENUS to protect their own world from the cosmic nuclear fallout that was causing their world to die. With our highly developed technology, it was proposed that a screen be erected above their atmosphere which could repel the cosmic rays, keeping the ozone levels, which is the same as ours, intact, allowing the substance of the world beneath to recover, on the understanding that the extraction of the earth's technology be suspended and travel restrictions be withdrawn until the screen installed and operating. Also to be requested was the dispensing of the sphere-cubes allowing a normal resumption of everyday activities.

The earth's scientists also agreed to assist the HOMOGENUS with the re-establishment of their lost ecosystems across the world, which would need considerable time and expertise spent on re-generating crops with improved farming methods involving training for the future generations of farmers. Excitement grew as the proposed date for the gathering of the world leaders and scientists with the HOMOGENUS drew ever closer. With bated breath, every informed person on earth gave themselves up to speculation of the results of the talks. The question on many lips was how much technology had we already lost and if what was left was sufficient to do the job of suspending a screen above the parallel world's atmosphere. What if this failed? One couldn't be too negative but remain confident of a solution, this solution to befriend and end the animosity of both the earth and the parallel world nobody ever knew existed. Time seemed to stand still as Steve and Juliet stayed glued to the secret world transmissions. Regular daily bulletins were made to encourage countries across the globe to remain resolute and not give up hope. Many languages were transmitted to many different people groups and there appeared to be an air of comradeship as differing signals were sent across the continents begging for allegiance to one another. As day followed day, the countdown began until, eventually, the agreed day arrived with the international/cosmic talks beginning. It took two days for the complete package from Earth's representatives to be laid bare for the HOMOGENUS to accept or refuse what was on offer, but finally, the offer was accepted on the grounds that the Earth's scientists must see the proposal through from beginning to end.

The entire world went mad with joy, with buntings being hung from building to building despite the snow and impromptu street gatherings declaring victory at the same time thanking the HOMOGENUS for their decision to accept Earth's proposals and the attempt to alleviate the situation that had held them in stalemate for so many weeks, but which now offered the chance to return to normal life and perhaps a far greater understanding between the world's populations and even to those on the other side of the cosmos previously unknown territory.

Earth's scientists were as good as their word removing the colossal amount of snow that had spread across the globe, bringing relief to many. Temperatures began to rise as the earth returned to its normal weather conditions for that time of the year. The HOMOGENUS released their grip on mankind by withdrawing the use of the sphere-cubes, and once more, the population were able to move around freely without being restrained. Although many of nature's habitats had been destroyed because of the snow, there were, however, some that had survived, and there was no lack of willing workers to make sure of their continued survival, furthering the progression of new life in these and many other debilitated areas of the world. Work had immediately begun on the production of the cosmic screens that would be erected and seen operating by the world's top scientists. They would be sent into space by shuttlecraft to be positioned into the HOMOGENUS's atmosphere, now visible, to prevent nuclear cosmic rays from outer space from penetrating onto their world's surface, destroying eco-systems which sustained life on their planet, destroying their gathered technology and leaving a dying planet. The work of rebuilding these systems with the assistance of Earth's scientists would be a mammoth task and would take longer to re-establish than the positioning of the cosmic radiation screens. The work involved could easily take many years of absorbing work and training of the next generation to achieve a healthy working planet again with the population of their world able to live and thrive once more. in the meanwhile, the screens were delivered, installed and adjusted for accuracy before being declared fully operational in resisting the nuclear rays proving that Earth's scientists had performed an exemplary task in the future of planet Earth.

The HOMOGENUS did extend a congratulatory word of gratitude to the world's governments and scientists that a satisfactory solution had been found, suggesting that in future, they would request assistance from another world rather than take by force whatever it was they thought was needed. A kind of neutrality had developed between the two worlds as information was given and, indeed, exchanged.